Hello Goldy!

Aimee Aryal

Illustrated by Katherine Sable

MASCOT
BOOKS

www.mascotbooks.com

It was a beautiful fall day at the
University of Minnesota.

Goldy was on his way to the Metrodome
to watch a football game.

Goldy walked onto Northrop Mall and
heard towards Northrop Auditorium.

He passed by a professor who waved,
"Hello Goldy!"

Goldy passed by classroom buildings
and stopped in front of Morrill Hall.

A woman who works inside said,
"Hello Goldy!"

Goldy walked by the Armory.

Some students standing outside waved,
"Hello Goldy!"

Goldy walked over to the
Williams Arena where the
Gophers play basketball.

Goldy passed in front of the
Mariucci Arena. A group of hockey fans
standing outside yelled, "Hello Goldy!"

It was almost time for the football game.
Goldy went to the McNamara Alumni
Center to catch a ride to the Metrodome.

Some alumni there remembered
Goldy from when they went to U of M.
They said, "Hello, again, Goldy!"

Finally, Goldy arrived at
the Metrodome.

As he rode his scooter onto the
football field, the crowd cheered,
"Let's Go Golden Gophers!"

Goldy watched the game from the
sidelines and cheered for the team.

The Gophers scored six points!
The quarterback shouted,
"Touchdown Goldy!"

At half-time the Minnesota Marching
Band performed on the field.

Goldy and the crowd listened to
"The Minnesota Rouser."

The Minnesota Golden Gophers
won the football game!

Goldy gave Coach Mason a high-five.
The coach said, "Great game Goldy!"

After the football game, Goldy was tired.
It had been a long day at the
University of Minnesota.

He walked home and climbed into bed.

"Goodnight Goldy."

For Anna and Maya, Elika and Arjan,
and all of Goldy's little fans. ~ AA

To my loving family and friends who have
always supported and encouraged me. ~ KS

Special thanks to:

David Lindquist

Glen Mason

The University of Minnesota Alumni Association is a 60,000-member organization with a mission of creating lifelong connections to alumni, students, parents, and friends of the University of Minnesota; advocating for educational excellence; and building pride, spirit and community. Activate your membership today by calling 1-800-UM-ALUMS or join online at www.alumni.umn.edu.

For information please contact Mascot Books,
P.O. Box 220157, Chantilly, VA 20153-0157.

ISBN: 0-9743442-4-9

Printed in the United States.

www.mascotbooks.com